MAP OF
FIRE ISLAND
1980

BRIDGE

GREAT SOUTH

NEW
INLET

BRICK
TOWER

FIRE ISLAND
LIGHT HOUSE

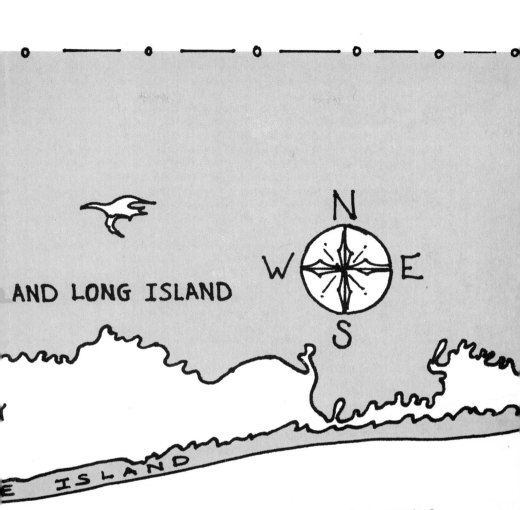

AND LONG ISLAND

ATLANTIC
OCEAN

E ISLAND

30³/₁₀ MILES

ROBERT'S TALL FRIEND

A Story of the Fire Island Lighthouse

BY VIVIAN FARRELL

Illustrated by
CHRISTY EDWARDS

ISLAND-METRO PUBLICATIONS, INC.
Plainview, Long Island, New York

Published by Island-Metro Publications Inc. - Book Publishing Division
Plainview, LI, NY 11803
First Printing - December, 1987

Printed on Long Island, USA by Lithographic Communications, Inc.
Ronkonkoma, LI, NY 11779

Library of Congress Cataloging-in-Publication Data

Farrell, Vivian.
  Robert's tall friend.

  Summary: Relates the story, based on fact, of how
a young boy's move to Fire Island, where his father is a
National Park Service Ranger, is strategic in the re-
storing to service of the island's crumbling old lighthouse.
  [1. Lighthouses—Fiction. 2. Fire Island (N.Y.)—
  Fiction] I. Edwards, Christy, ill. II. Title.
  PZ7.F24612Ro 1987   [Fic]   87-35246
          ISBN 0-9619832-0-5

For T.H.L.

CAPE HATTERAS,
North Carolina

CAPE LOOKOUT,
North Carolina

"...each lighthouse has a different design so that in the daytime ships can know

6

ASSATEAGUE
ISLAND,
Virginia

FIRE ISLAND, New York

...ne lighthouse from another," Robert's father explained.

A Note From the Author

This story is based on a time in the life of a real boy named Robert Norris.

During the years of the late 1970's and early 1980's, Robert lived with his father, Rockwell Norris, a National Park Service Ranger, and his mother, Audrey Norris, in the lightkeeper's cottage next to the Fire Island Lighthouse at Fire Island, off the south shore of Long Island, New York.

In this story, I cannot promise that all the adventures in Robert's life did indeed take place as I have written them. What is real and what is fantasy is up to you, the reader, to decide. But one thing is true and important: the need for us to keep forever the beauty and majesty of our past that the Fire Island Lighthouse represents.

V.F.

CHAPTER 1

Curled up in the back seat of the car, clutching a pillow, it seemed to Robert as if the road had gone on and on without end. He thought again of his best friend Timmy, back home, missing him already. And then he nodded off to sleep.

The only good thing about moving was that their new home would be a lighthouse right on the ocean. One of his books had a picture of a lighthouse, out on a tip of land, shining its beam to a ship in a storm.

Robert's father was a park ranger and had said to him when they were packing, "Son, it's a great place for a boy to grow up."

Now his father's hand touched his back. Robert stirred and realized the car had stopped.

"We're almost there, Robert. I thought I'd wake you before we get on the bridge. You can see the lighthouse from here."

Robert uncurled his legs, rubbed his eyes and sat up.

His father had a map spread out and was showing his mother Fire Island, a long, skinny stretch of land like a shoelace.

"There she is," he pointed to the lighthouse on the map. "She used to be on the tip of the island, marking the dangerous inlet where the ocean tides came into the

bay. But the waves have carried sand westward for five miles beyond the lighthouse and the inlet is over here now." He ran his finger over the map to the new inlet and pointed out of the window to the west.

So *our* lighthouse isn't up on rocks at the tip of an island, Robert thought.

The car moved ahead over a long bridge, arching high over the water. Robert could see the low strip of island with the lighthouse looking like a tiny, dark finger pointing to the sky. The water was shining in the late summer sun as they reached the island and circled past a brick tower, heading toward the lighthouse. Soon they were bumping along a sandy road and Robert's eyes grew larger as the lighthouse seemed to grow in size.

"Daddy, why is it black and white striped?" he asked.

"Well, I read that this lighthouse used to be pale yellow. Then in the 1890's they coated it with tar. But it was too dark so they painted on two bands of white leaving two of black," Robert's father explained. "And in 1912 a cement coating was put on and painted with the same design. Today each lighthouse has a different design so that in the daytime ships can know one lighthouse from another."

They were getting near enough to see the windows at the top. He could climb up there and look out. What a great place to live!

Robert studied the lighthouse. It looked like a giant chess piece standing tall. It even had a crown. It must be the queen in the chess set. The bottom flares out like a skirt!

But as they got really close he sensed that something was terribly wrong. The lighthouse was full of cracks. Big chunks of the black and white cement coating had fallen off, exposing red bricks underneath.

The car turned toward the high stone wall of the platform on which the lighthouse and a gray stone building sat.

"It looks awful," Robert's mother said. "Is it safe?"

"She's not going to fall over," Robert's father said. "She hasn't been cared for, but she's very well built. This lighthouse has been standing since 1858, through many a hurricane. Some day I'll take you to the top. It's a long climb."

"Some day!" Robert was crushed. He wanted to go up right away.

"Here we are," his father said. "Our new home." The car stopped.

Together they climbed a steep wooden stair to the level of the stone platform on which the lighthouse and the other building stood. Robert realized that he had misunderstood. They weren't going to live *in* the lighthouse at all. They were going to live in the stone house beside it. "*At* the Fire Island Lighthouse," his father had said.

There was an arched porch over the front door but Robert's father had a key for a side door. They went in and explored, first the downstairs. There was a fireplace in the living room.

"This is where the lightkeeper's family used to gather in the cold winter days," Robert's father said.

Robert ran upstairs to explore and looked out all the windows.

From the front windows he could see ocean waves crashing against the beach and there were high, white sand hills his mother called "dunes" that looked as if they would be great fun to slide down. Then from the back windows, the view of calm bay water lapping up to thick marsh grass, was almost blocked by the lighthouse. Commanding Robert's attention, the tall tower seemed to say to him, "Look at me, standing here."

They unpacked the car, carrying load after load up the wooden steps and into the house.

"Come on, let's explore a little. We can unpack after dark," Robert's mother said. The sun was a big orange ball over the bridge.

They crossed the sand road and went through a gap in the dunes to look at the surf. Robert watched a while and then started to climb a dune behind his parents. What a great place to slide!

"Robert!" his father called sharply. "Don't do that! You must *never* go on the dunes. It's against the law!"

His father explained that the grass growing on the dunes kept the sand from blowing away in the strong winds. It was very important not to disturb the dune grass.

"My job here is to guard the sand dunes, tend the beaches, and protect everything that grows in this area, birds and animals too. Some birds make their nests right on the ground. There are rabbits and fox and turtles and even deer out there." He pointed out toward the low wind-bent trees and high bushes. Robert thought about the fun he'd have tramping through the bushes looking for deer. Some of the pines had great hollows of sand underneath.

"There's a great place to build a fort!" Robert said, pointing to a huge pine branch the wind had blown into an arching shape.

"Robert, you have to be very careful about where you walk here," his mother said. "There is poison ivy almost

Together they climbed a steep wooden stair to the level of the stone platform on which the lighthouse and the other building stood.

everywhere." She was a nurse and had seen some bad cases of the itchy rash.

Robert's father explained, "Poison ivy is one of the plants that is important to keep the sand from blowing away. See, here is poison ivy turning red." He pointed to three-leaved branches with clusters of berries. They were more like bushes than ivy vines. So Robert couldn't tramp around wherever he wanted to.

Robert looked up to see a bird that Dad said was a herring gull. It cried as it wheeled overhead. It was a sad sound. Robert called to it, "Don't cry."

"What's that you said?" his father asked.

Robert shrugged: "Just answering the bird."

His mother laughed and said, "You certainly have a great imagination!"

They turned to go back to their new home and it was nearly dark. Robert looked up at the top of the lighthouse and was disappointed that there was no light. "Dad, where's the light? Aren't you going to turn it on?"

"No, Son. The beacon was turned off in 1974," Robert's father explained. "No one takes care of the lighthouse. It just isn't needed any more."

"A lighthouse that doesn't light," Robert said quietly. "That's sad."

"It is," his mother said.

"It used to be important," said his father. "Ships coming from Europe to New York would see its light and know they had reached America. This was the first beacon that welcomed them. Now ships have radar and electronics to guide them. The light isn't needed."

Robert looked up at the old lighthouse with its cracks and broken windows. He felt a strange ache deep inside as he walked to the house and up to his room.

15

CHAPTER II

Next morning a small yellow school bus came to pick up Robert. It was more like a high station wagon.

He waved to his mother who would be driving back over the bridge to the mainland to her nursing job. She was dressed all in white and his father wore his Ranger uniform with a "Smokey-the-Bear" hat.

"Have a good day!" they called.

Down the sandy road and then over a cut in the dunes the little four-wheel-drive bus drove onto the beach. What fun to ride along and watch the surf!

They picked up five other children on the way to the school in the village of Ocean Beach. Robert was careful to tell them that he lived *at* the lighthouse. He felt ashamed about how shabby the Fire Island Lighthouse had turned out to be.

He wanted to invite someone to play after school but he found out it was too far to walk and there were strict rules against driving along the beach. So on his way back to his new home, he was alone again in the bus, thinking about his best friend, Timmy.

"Lighthouse," the driver called out, grinning. "Last stop. Anyone for the lighthouse?"

Robert didn't find it funny as he jumped down into the sand.

He was all alone. There was just the sound of the waves

Robert looked up at the old lighthouse with its cracks and broken windows. He felt a strange ache deep inside as he walked to the house and up to his room.

crashing against the shore.

Up the steps he climbed and went in the kitchen door, dumping his books on the table. He poked in the refrigerator, poured a glass of milk and lined up four cookies on the table. He broke them apart, then nibbled carefully at the plain sides first, saving the icing sides for last.

"Well," he asked himself, "What now? There may be things to do but it's no fun here by myself." He sighed. "I wish I had a friend."

CHAPTER III

Robert was glad his mother came home from work early the next day. They went picking beach plums which were like clusters of purplish cherries with long stems. Robert discovered they had hard round seeds in the center when he tasted one. It was so sour he spit it out.

His mother laughed and said, "But they make wonderful jelly, Robert, the best!" She carried a big scrub pail and Robert had the small plastic one he used for gathering shells. They both wore jeans tucked in high socks to protect their ankles from poison ivy.

Near the beach plums were other bushes with narrower leathery leaves and clusters of tiny gray berries on their branches. They felt waxy and his mother explained how the Pilgrims used them to make candles: "They gathered thousands of bayberries and boiled them in water to melt the wax off. When the water cooled there was a layer of wax on the top. The candles smelled like this." She crushed one of the bayberry leaves and held it to Robert's nose. He liked the spicy clean smell.

They were crossing a low, wet area to reach other beach plum bushes. Robert heard his mother call out and saw her bend down.

"Look! Cranberries!" She held the lacy, green leaves aside and quickly picked a handful. Robert dumped his bucket of plums into his mother's and they used his bucket for cranberries. It was like "finding rubies in the grass," his

"Lighthouse," the bus driver called, but Robert was already at the bus door. He ran for the house . . . .

20

mother said.

They picked for nearly an hour talking about many things—his old school, kids at his new school, and his letter from Timmy, still his best friend.

Next week would be his birthday and he had hardly started to ask about a party when his mother quickly agreed, "Robert, it's a great idea. But I don't want you to be disappointed. You know your school friends can't drive back and forth along the beach. Maybe we can find someone else to invite." Their buckets were nearly full.

Suddenly she said, "I have an idea. There's a nurse I work with who told me she has twin boys. They're your age too. I'm pretty sure she'd drive them over the bridge for a party. How does that sound? Let's plan it! I'll take that day off so we can have a homemade cake."

"Great!" Robert put his arm around his mother's waist.

As they walked back to the house they planned games for the party, some outside and some in. It was too windy for his badminton set. But frisbees might be fun, and kite flying.

They put their buckets, brimming with berries, on the kitchen counter.

That weekend they shopped on the mainland for party prizes and candy.

The morning of the party they blew up balloons until they were out of breath. Then he went off to school happily, looking forward to coming home in the afternoon. He wouldn't be lonely this day—no sir!

"Lighthouse," the bus driver called, but Robert was already at the bus door. He ran for the house and saw that there was no extra car outside. Maybe the guests came by boat.

He ran into the house and his mother said, "Here's the birthday boy!" Robert's father was home too and they both hugged him. Then his mother said, "I'm afraid there's bad news. The twins' mother called. They both came down with chicken pox. But we'll have fun ourselves. Dad came home early. We'll play all the games and have the cake with candles..."

Robert felt like crying but he didn't want to act like a baby. Yet he couldn't stop a salty tear that trickled down his cheek.

"I'm so sorry, so sorry, dear," his mother kept murmuring.

"Come on, Robert," his father said suddenly, taking his hand. "I want to take you and Mom up in the lighthouse. It's your birthday. Let's go and see the inside and climb to the top."

Robert brightened right away. He was going up in the lighthouse. Great!

They went out and around to the back where a high chain-link fence kept people away from pieces falling off the lighthouse.

There was a heavy, wooden door set back in an arched opening at the base of the tower. His father tugged at the handle. It stuck first, then the door creaked open.

They stepped inside a short brick tunnel.

"The walls here are ten feet thick," Robert's father said.

There was a winding staircase with pie shaped steps made of rusting iron in a pattern of holes. Robert looked up through the steps which seemed to go up and around, up and around forever.

"Don't look up," his father said. "There are always chips of paint and rust falling and you'll get something in your eye. Stay together."

He led the way, grasping a rope that was attached through metal loops to the flaking brick walls. Robert was starting to count the steps. He had heard there were 192. At the 26th step there was a landing and a window. It was very dirty and the wind blew through three broken panes. But they could look west toward the brick water tower of the state park.

They stopped to catch their breath and see a wonderful high view at three other landings. Then they went up steps that were more like a ladder and through a trap door to a room shaped like a half-circle, lighted by a big arched window.

Up they climbed again on another ladder stair to a completely round room. "This is the watch room," his father explained. "Here's where the lightkeeper stayed up all night. In the days before electricity this is where he kept extra oil for the big light. First they used whale oil and finally kerosene."

Robert's father paused in the little circular space with round portholes of light before the next metal ladder. (Twelve steps, Robert counted.)

Now they were in another round, empty room. "This is the gallery room," Robert's father said as he walked over to a little, low door and opened it.

He bent his head and pointed outward, saying, "This goes to the gallery, a walkway all around the lighthouse."

Robert's mother was nervous. "I'll stay inside. Heights make me dizzy," she said.

The ranger and his son stepped out into the wind. Robert grasped the railing tightly as he stood close to his dad. He loved the feeling of the wind blowing his hair straight back; it was almost like flying! His birthday disappointment was forgotten.

They watched the ocean and bay far below and saw the island stretch out and get narrow in the distance. They were higher than some birds flying by!

23

Robert felt like crying but he didn't want to act like a baby.

"Listen carefully, Son," his father shouted against the wind. "Never walk out on the gallery unless I'm with you."

Robert understood that it was dangerous. But his father seemed to be saying he would be allowed to climb the lighthouse again *by himself* now that he was ten years old!

"Let's go on to the top." Robert's mother called from the doorway.

They came in and went up another ladder stair. (Nine steps, this time.)

They were up to the top, in the lantern room. Even though it was dirty and the wind whistled through broken glass panes, he could see very far on all sides. There was the dock where he and his mom fished for snappers. The water looked wrinkled and the boats were like toys. The road seemed like a tan snake through the greenness below.

It was the most exciting moment of Robert's life. He felt like the king of the world! This was much better than the tree house he and Timmy had built. Robert was going to climb here again and again, way up to these four one-on-top-of-the-other rooms!

But when they finally started winding down, clinking on the rusty steps, Robert felt sad about how old and dirty and empty the lighthouse was.

"Thanks for the visit, Lighthouse," he called back as they went out the door and back to the cottage.

Robert's parents smiled to each other as his mother hugged him and said, "That's my Robert—wonderful imagination!"

Robert sometimes played chess with his father. But that night the three of them played Monopoly. Robert tried to be cheerful but deep inside him there was an emptiness that would not go away.

He felt as empty as the useless, old lighthouse.

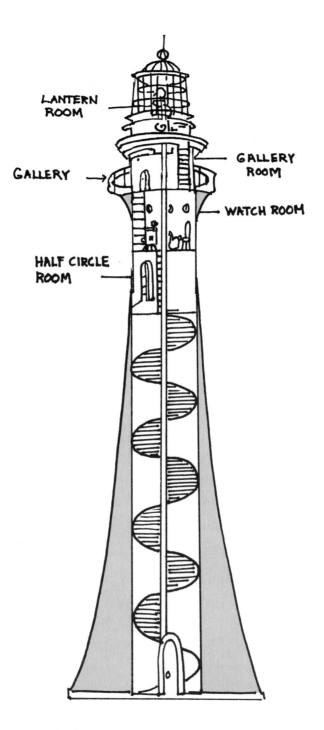

LANTERN ROOM

GALLERY

GALLERY ROOM

WATCH ROOM

HALF CIRCLE ROOM

Robert was going to climb here again and again, way up to these four one-on-top-of-the-other rooms!

CHAPTER IV

The following day after school, Robert was beachcombing, walking along with his pail, finding shells and frosted beach glass for his collection. He loved to watch the groups of sandpipers, those funny little birds that ran along the beach, never getting their feet wet as the waves washed back and forth. They looked like wind-up toys.

He sat down to examine his catch: a fluted scallop, nearly perfect with tan and brown stripes, two boat shells with their little seats inside, a rather large moonsnail swirled to a "tiger's-eye" on the outside and so smooth inside. Three clamshells had purple spots. His mother told him the Indians made money beads from them. Another sea clam was nearly big enough for his mother to use for a soap dish.

Robert was beginning to enjoy finding things to do by himself. He put his shells carefully back into his bucket and his eye caught what looked like a really big, round moonsnail being washed in by a wave. He ran to grab it before it could be carried back out and he got his shoes wet. It wasn't a shell. It was a quite nice rubber ball with fading red stripes. Wouldn't it be fun to play catch with someone!

He threw the ball into the air and caught it. Then he threw it higher and laughed as the wind blew it away from him and he had to run to catch it. He was playing catch with the wind!

He threw it still higher and, as he watched it fall, his eye caught some movement in the top of the lighthouse. There it was again, a fluttery movement like the sleeve of a shirt.

A ghost! He wondered. No! He didn't believe in spooks. But there *was* something.

He walked toward the lighthouse, shading his eyes with his hand and trying to look into the lantern room way on top. He had to find out what was up there. When he reached the heavy wooden door he turned the handle with both hands and pulled it as his father had yesterday. It creaked open. He was proud he did it by himself. He stepped inside, telling himself there was nothing to be afraid of.

"Anybody here?" Robert called, but his voice was hardly more than a whisper.

He tried again louder, "Anybody here?" His voice echoed from the curved walls.

He put one foot on the first step of the winding staircase, then his other foot on the next step, pausing to listen as he climbed higher.

Once he thought he heard a little noise way up over his head. Otherwise he only heard the pounding of his own heart. He kept climbing up, up, determined to solve the mystery. He reached the half-circle room and the first ladder stair to the watch room. Then the next ladder to the gallery room.

He heard nothing but the wind.

He climbed five steps of the last ladder until his eyes peered over the top of the metal floor of the lantern room.

"Why, it's a bird!" he said aloud. It was perched on a window ledge looking very frightened with one drooping wing. The wind whistled through the broken window of the lantern room.

Robert moved very slowly.

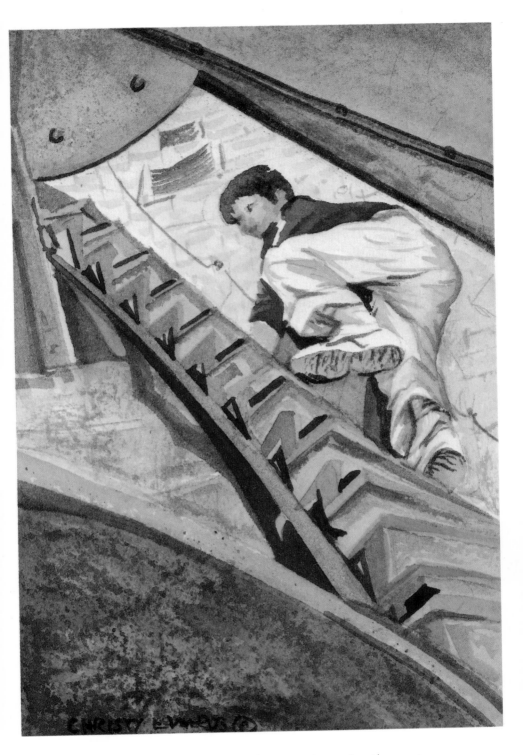

He kept climbing up, up, determined to solve the mystery.

29

"Poor bird." It flopped down onto the floor. "You've hurt your wing."

Slowly Robert took off his jacket as he had seen his father once do to catch a frightened bird.

Robert went closer. Very slowly and carefully, he reached out and then, in one motion, laid the jacket over the bird and picked it up. He could feel its tiny heart pounding. He folded back the jacket from its head and held the bird to his chest with one arm.

"I'll help you," he said, knowing it would be hard to climb down with only one free hand. The wind moaning around the lighthouse sounded like a voice. Robert thought he heard it say, "Now help *me*, help *meeeee*."

As he struggled down the ladders and circled all the way down the steps he thought he heard that cry again in the wind.

He took the bird to the kitchen of the cottage and put it with some soft rags in an empty box on the floor. He held it still while he talked to it. "There now. You can rest," he told the little creature as he covered the box with a light cloth. He knew that if it could rest, its wing would get better soon.

He took off his wet shoes and socks and rinsed them off in the sink.

"My shoes are salty wet," he explained to the bird. "They have to be rinsed with fresh water or Mom says they'll never dry right."

He hummed softly as he tiptoed about in his bare feet. He felt good. He had a pet! The bird would get to know him and they'd be the best of friends.

He was sure his parents would be happy for him. He had heard them talking one night when they thought he was asleep. His mother had said, "He needs a kitten or a puppy—something to love and cuddle and keep him company."

His father had agreed: "I know, but a cat might stalk the birds that I'm here to protect, and a dog would chase the rabbits and deer. You know I can't let that happen." Robert had heard his mother's sigh.

Well, now he had his pet. Just wait until they came home and found out. How glad they'd be!

A little time had passed and now he raised a corner of the cloth cover and peeked at his new pet. "I'll have to find a name for you," he said softly. "I can't just call you 'Bird.'"

He heard his mother coming in the door and turned around to hide the box from sight. He started to tell her his news. But before he'd said five words, his father came in, too.

"Good!" Robert said, clapping his hands. "I can tell you both! Wait till you see what I have."

He proudly told the whole story of how he discovered the wounded bird. Then he took the cloth cover off the box.

His father reached in and lifted the bird with both hands. He examined it carefully all over saying, "Its wing is not broken. It was scared and worn out when you found it. I'm proud of you Robert. It wouldn't have been able to get out of the lantern room by itself."

Robert smiled, feeling pleased.

"This bird is a barn swallow," his father said. "See, it has a forked tail like a V in the middle. It was flying south for the winter."

"So that's what my pet bird is," Robert said.

He saw his father and mother look at each other. His father put a hand on Robert's shoulder and looked into his eyes. "Robert, you can't call him yours."

Robert felt his heart sink. "Why not? I saved him! So whose bird is he?"

He took the bird to the kitchen of the cottage and put it with some soft rags in an empty box on the floor. He held it still while he talked to it. "There now. You can rest," he told the little creature . . . .

"Son, this may be hard to understand, but this is a wild bird. He belongs to nature."

Robert shook his head back and forth. "But you said he would have died..."

"I know. You rescued him from that. You did very well. But when his strength returns, we have to let him go free." His father pointed to the outdoors. "There is his home. That's where he belongs...where he'll be happy."

Robert fought back tears. Why didn't anything go right? Why couldn't he ever have a friend?

Aloud he asked, "Can I keep him in my room just for tonight? Please?"

His father agreed.

Robert took Bird upstairs. They could be together for this one night. In bed he lay awake for a long time, talking to Bird about all the things he had wanted to do and couldn't.

He finally said, "Goodnight, Bird."

Robert fell asleep, longing for a friend.

CHAPTER V

Early the next morning Robert and his father let the bird go. They watched it for a long time as it flew away.

"Be happy, Bird," Robert called as the bird became a dot against the sky.

"I'm sure it will be, thanks to you, Son," his father said, putting his comforting arm around Robert's shoulders. He pointed up high to some hawks flying west.

Robert had learned that Fire Island was on the main "flyway" for migrating birds that come from far north in Canada. There was a pond near the lighthouse and hundreds of birds stopped for water on their way south. Robert was learning lots of their names.

His father had shown him on the map.

"They fly south from New England over Long Island Sound. Then they fly south over Long Island and Great South Bay. When they get to Fire Island they sense that there is nothing south except open ocean so they must fly west to find more land," his father had said.

Robert told about Bird at school that day. He explained how wild birds belong to nature and can't be pets. He wasn't lonely until he came home again in the afternoon. After his snack he went outside just looking around. Maybe Bird would come back!

Many of the bushes were turning red. His father said the fiery fall color was one of the reasons Fire Island may have gotten its name. That and the fact that, before the lighthouse, people used to light fires on the beach to warn ships.

There were white clouds moving swiftly overhead. The marsh grass dipped and swayed with a rustling sound. Suddenly he remembered he had left his bucket of shells on the beach yesterday. He ran to the beach and found the bucket with the shells just where he left it, but he couldn't find his ball. The tide was coming up higher and the sand was blowing so hard it stung his legs.

As he walked back he found himself staring at the lighthouse. There it stood, of no use at all. Nothing to do, he thought, just like me.

The wind was pushing from the ocean and it seemed to Robert that his legs started walking towards the lighthouse all by themselves. Next thing he knew, he was pulling open the heavy wooden door. It was good to be in out of the wind!

Once again he started to climb the curving metal steps, not hurrying this time and not counting, just taking time to see everything. He noticed spider webs between the steps. He put his hand out and touched the wall. It felt cold and the white paint flaked and fell like snow.

"Needs new paint," he said aloud.

He stopped at each landing. Nearly every landing window had a broken pane.

He climbed past the half-circle room to the watch room with its three porthole windows. He tried to imagine what it must have been like when the lightkeeper stayed there. His father said he had a stove to keep warm in winter and heat his coffee—he had to stay awake all night. The wind was moaning again. The lightkeeper must have been lonely up here.

He climbed to the next room above and glanced at the little, low door leading outside to the gallery. Robert remembered his father's warning.

Now, up the last ladder to the lantern room. There it was, the great beacon lamp. The metal had turned black and the glass needed cleaning. He looked through the dusty windows. He could see the ocean surf swelling and breaking. He could see the island, stretching out of sight in one direction with little dots of houses far off. When he looked the opposite way, towards New York City, he saw the brick tower and the bridge to the mainland, and then the usually calm Great South Bay, which today the wind was whipping up and decorating with whitecaps that reminded him of peaks of icing on his birthday cake.

"Some view," he said aloud to the moaning wind and immediately he heard a cry, a sob, and he turned quickly.

"Who's there?" he asked, startled.

Then he heard very clearly the words, "Help me!"

This was the same sound he'd heard yesterday when he found Bird. He listened breathlessly, wondering how wind could sound like words.

"Help meeee." Again, but faint this time.

It had to be a trick of the wind, he decided, and his thoughts jumped to other things. He had an idea.

He clattered down the spiral stair, out of the lighthouse and into the cottage, and gathered cleaning things from the kitchen: his mother's bucket, some rags and brass cleaner. He put a plastic bottle full of soapy water in the bucket and carried a broom in the same hand. He had suddenly thought if he cleaned up a room in the lighthouse, it would be a perfect playroom for him all his own. And the view would be better if a window or two were clear.

Looping the bucket over his shoulder, once again he

When he looked the opposite way, towards New York City, he saw the brick tower and the bridge to the mainland. . . .

climbed all the lighthouse stairs. When he reached the lantern room and caught his breath, he started to sweep the floor, coughing with the dust. Then he cleaned a window as high as he could reach. Now he had one good, clear place to look through. He saw a ship far in the distance, moving steadily through the rough ocean. He wished he could turn on the light and flash a greeting to it.

"Welcome to America!" he would say.

He tried the polish on the metal and rubbed and rubbed a spot the size of a quarter until it gleamed like gold.

"Aaahhh." He heard a voice. "Better. Feels better."

He looked about in alarm. The wind was howling now, but he was sure he had heard a voice, too.

"Who's talking?" he asked.

"Save me, Robert. Please save me."

Now the voice was clear above the wind. A woman's kind of voice.

"Who is it? How do you know my name?"

Instead of answering, the voice moaned, "I need a friend."

Robert found himself answering, "I do, too."

"Help meeee!" the voice pleaded.

Robert shook his head to make sure he heard clearly. Was it the wind or just his imagination? But, all at once, something came over him. It was a feeling and an understanding at the same time. It was something that seemed magical and it felt good. It didn't scare him, but it made him sad because... now he knew. Yes, he knew it was the lighthouse herself, hurting and pleading for help because her insides and outsides were peeling and crumbling.

He didn't know how he knew, he just knew; and it seemed right to say to her, "Lighthouse, don't cry. I'm here and I care about you."

This time it didn't surprise Robert when the lighthouse answered. She spoke clearly now. "Oh, Robert, I feel quite ill. My insides pain me. Outside my cement skin is burning and peeling. My spiral stairs are rusting, and oh, my poor lantern room has a headache. Thank you for sweeping and polishing; it felt so good. But I need more, paint and repairs—and most of all I need my light to shine. Please help me, Robert!"

Robert twisted the rag in his hands. He understood but he felt helpless. "Lighthouse, I want to help you, but I'm just a boy and I don't know how."

"You will know soon, Robert," said the lighthouse with a sure voice. "You are very special. I have chosen you. I know you'll find a way."

He was tired that night from all his cleaning and climbing but he fell asleep quickly with a better feeling than he'd had in a long time.

At last he had a friend...but what a friend! The lighthouse herself! No one would believe him. He must keep it a secret that she could speak. So he held it in his heart and told no one.

When he reached the lantern room and caught his breath, he started to sweep the floor . . . .

CHAPTER VI

In the next weeks, Robert came to know every inch of the lighthouse. He loved the four one-on-top-of-the-other rooms.

He brought his collection of shells and beach glass to the half-circle room and spread them out like an exhibit, including his "lucky charm." That was the piece of concrete that had fallen from the lighthouse one day, landing right in his pail!

His favorite place was the lantern room where he had his talks with his new friend, the lighthouse. It was like being right inside her head.

As the days passed, her voice grew surer and stronger. Sometimes he thought he saw a faint flicker in her light as she told him so many stories of when she was young. Robert was happy with his new friend, but he also felt sad that he could not help her more.

One day Robert asked about the circle of gray stones on the ground to the west of the lighthouse.

"Robert, my friend, that was my father, a shorter lighthouse than I. He was torn down when a taller lighthouse was needed to warn the ships that they were nearing land. You see, they were running aground because they couldn't see my father's light soon enough. He was only 74 feet high. And so they built me! I am 168 feet tall," she said proudly.

From the lantern room window, Robert stared down at the strange circle and wondered what the old father-lighthouse was like.

"From some of those stones the workmen built the house where you live. It makes me feel good to have the stones of my father close by."

"Did your tallness save the ships from trouble?" Robert asked.

In that proud voice she said, "Oh, yes! They saw my light from far away. Fewer ships were wrecked and many lives saved after I started beaming. I also had special lenses invented by a Frenchman named Fresnel. They made my light stronger and brighter before I had electricity."

Did Robert really see the light flickering as she spoke or was it a reflection of the sun?

She went on: "And in storms, people who lived far down the beach came all the way here for shelter. I always felt like a mother hen gathering her chicks. I was the safest place. Some of their houses were washed away by the waves," she sighed. "And the little boats on the bay always looked for my light to lead them to one shore or another. But now they think I'm not needed. They have that newfangled blinker light up on the brick tower."

She was quiet for a while and Robert guessed that she wanted to rest. He went down to the watch room where he had left his books and did his homework.

When he finished he tiptoed up to the lantern room.

"Are you rested?" he asked. "I want to ask you a question."

"What is it, Robert?"

There was a moment of silence and then he asked, "Do

you think they still need you?"

"Oh my! What a question!" she said. She took some time to answer. "Yes, Robert, I know they need me. I can tell the ocean ships miss my friendly beams when they pass. My beams used to go 20 miles. The little boats on the bay can't see the blinker light. It aims only out to sea. So what are the little boats to do? They need me too. I should be beaming forever! I never get tired! I was so upset when they turned off my light! Oh Robert, I'm over 125 years old. Sometimes I want to give up and let them tear me down the way they did my father!"

Then her courage returned and she said firmly, "No! No, Robert. I should be repaired. It can be done! I should be beaming! My light must be turned on again!"

"Oh, how I wish I could help," Robert said. "How I wish." But he still didn't understand what he could do.

He brought his collection of shells and beach glass to the half-circle room and spread them out like an exhibit, including his "lucky charm."

CHAPTER VII

One day the next week a terrible storm raged while they were at school and the children had to bend their heads low against the fierce wind as they made their way to the bus. As the children were dropped off, adults were there to help them get home.

Robert thought of the lighthouse and hoped she was all right. His father said she had weathered many storms, even hurricanes, but maybe that was when she was younger and stronger.

Crashing waves sprayed the windows of the bus and it swayed as it fought its way along the beach. Finally he reached his stop.

The driver didn't joke today. He was very serious as he warned, "Better go to the house and stay indoors. And keep away from that crumbling, old lighthouse!"

It hurt Robert to think that the driver called his lighthouse old and crumbling. As he climbed the wooden stairs to the stone platform, all he could think of was that the lighthouse might need him.

He ran past the house directly to her and shouted above the howling wind, "Lighthouse! Lighthouse, can you hear me? Are you all right?"

He could scarcely see as his eyes clouded with tears and the rain beat against his face. The sky grew blacker and a great gust of wind whipped from the ocean. Lightning flashed with a loud crack of thunder.

A chunk of cement tore loose from the side of the lighthouse, tumbling down right towards Robert. Terrified, he leaped aside and it barely missed his head. The chunk hit his leg and threw him to the ground. He grabbed his thigh, screaming in pain. It was a double pain: his wound and the fact that the lighthouse had struck him.

His mother's car pulled into the roadway and she ran up the stairs just as his father came from the other direction.

His father lifted him up carefully and his mother ran to hold the door open, shouting, "Hurry, he's bleeding. Oh, Robert! You could have been killed!"

His father struggled into the house and put Robert down on the couch. His voice was angry, "That lighthouse *is* dangerous!"

Robert's mother ripped away the rest of the leg of his jeans saying, "I hate that lighthouse! It almost killed our boy. It's got to be torn down!"

"Right to the ground," his father added, "and I'm going to make sure that it's done, so she never hurts anyone again."

"No! No! You can't do that!" cried Robert. His mother was cleaning his wound but it hardly hurt. What he did feel was the pain that his friend, the lighthouse, was in danger.

His parents didn't understand. The lighthouse had not meant to hurt him, he was sure. She couldn't help what happened.

Robert cried out, "You can't tear down a lighthouse that has saved so many ships and lives! The boats on the bay still need her. The ships on the sea miss her. Everyone says she's old and crumbling. But it's not fair to tear her down or let her fall to pieces. You should hear the way she cries when I talk to her. She tells me she's in pain! She wants to be fixed

46

up."

He was sobbing now. His parents could hardly believe their ears.

"She told me her story so many times," Robert continued, "how she was built after they tore down her lighthouse-father...how this house we live in was made from his old, gray stones...how her beams used to show ships in storms where the beach was...Oh, she told me so much."

Robert reached for his father's handkerchief to wipe his eyes.

Struggling for control, he went on: "Mom, Dad! Just think. The lighthouse told me she could be repaired and her light made to shine again. And maybe one day kids could come and visit her and our house, too and ...OUCH!"

Robert's mother was taping the edges of his cut together with butterfly bandages.

"Hold on there, Son," his father said. "Let Mother fix your leg. You're very upset. I don't think you know what you're saying."

"Listen, Robert," his mother said. "You were almost killed. You're lucky to have only this cut on your leg. Do you realize you were saying that the lighthouse has been talking to you?"

"Oh, Mom," Robert said. "I was never going to tell anybody. I promised myself and the lighthouse that I'd keep it a secret. But now I guess I have to tell what I know to save her life."

Robert's parents looked at each other. He saw them nod as if agreeing that he needed to keep talking.

Robert was glad they were listening. He went on, trying to make them understand that he really had been talking with the lighthouse for weeks. He really heard her talk back to him. He wanted to tell them all he had learned in their talks—

His father lifted him up carefully....

the wrecks, the hurricanes, and the great fire that burned nearly the whole end of the island.

Robert went on, "There was once a big hotel nearby where hundreds of people came in a paddle-wheel steamer. The lighthouse watched them play on the beach and she could hear the music at night when they were dancing! There were lots of other children who lived at this lighthouse and even a baby was born here!"

He told them how the lighthouse felt as she watched, year after year, while the wind and the waves carried the sand west so that the island grew before her very eyes and she was no longer at the tip of Fire Island.

Breathlessly he finished with the lighthouse's dream of being made like new again, just as she was long ago, inside and outside, so she would stand beautiful and strong again. And their house, the lightkeeper's cottage, would be a quiet place, like a museum, for people to visit and study and learn. Then, visitors could climb the winding stairs of the lighthouse to the very top where the big lamp would beam out on the bay and ocean once more.

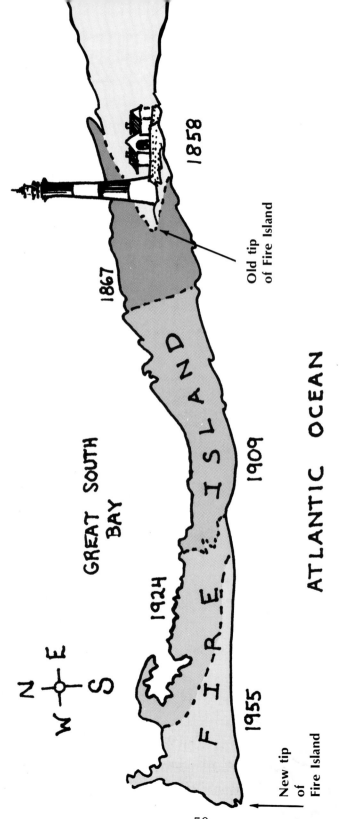

GREAT SOUTH BAY

F · I · R · E I · S · L · A · N · D

1924

1909

1955

New tip of Fire Island

1867

1858

Old tip of Fire Island

ATLANTIC OCEAN

N
W — E
S

He told them how the lighthouse felt as she watched, year after year, while the wind and the waves carried the sand west so that the island grew before her very eyes and she was no longer at the tip of Fire Island.

50

CHAPTER VIII

When Robert finished, a strange thing happened. His father, so angry earlier, became quiet and thoughtful.

Robert saw his mother's eyes widen. She said, "His facts seem to be correct."

He saw her look at his father as she said slowly, "Maybe the lighthouse *could* be repaired and relighted."

Then both parents smiled.

"What an idea!" His father nodded. "The lighthouse all brand new...those powerful beams circling in the night again. And a place for people to visit here in this house...a seashore exhibit. It's fantastic!"

He gave his son a hug: "Son, you're a genius! What a beautiful place this could be! So many people could come and see this glorious National Seashore and visit *your* lighthouse!"

"Think of the field trips," his mother added. "Whole classes could come to learn about whales, shipwrecks, things that grow on the beach, especially the history of the lighthouse! Oh, Robert! I'm so proud of you."

"No, no," Robert protested. "It's not me. It isn't my idea. The lighthouse thought of it. She kept telling me about this while I was talking to her."

Robert's father seemed so excited now about fixing up the lighthouse, the restoration idea, that he didn't question again whether Robert did or did not have talks with the lighthouse.

He snapped his fingers and said, "I know just the people to talk to, boaters and old timers, people who'll raise money to make this happen. And Robert, you're right about the boats on the bay needing the light. Some of them don't have fancy electronic equipment. And that strobe light that blinks on the brick tower *doesn't* shine on the bay side."

Robert's mother seemed caught up in the excitement as she added, "Lighthouses are an important part of history. They're sort of grand and royal and lovely. Just looking at them reminds us of days of glory in our history. People need that. We've got to save our lighthouse!"

"Yes," said his father. "It's a little like preserving the ancient pyramids of Egypt."

"And the Great Wall of China," Robert chimed in, struggling to sit up. He clapped his hands as he thought of another: "And what about the Statue of Liberty!"

And so, all that rainy, stormy afternoon, Robert, his mother and his father excitedly planned how they would get everything started to save the lighthouse.

The storm died down, and the sun came out before it set.

The next day Robert's father called many people and went to see others. And when he came home he said they all liked the idea. They all knew it would cost a lot of money, probably over a million dollars, but people would give money to help because it was important.

Robert's mother and father told everyone that it was all Robert's idea, and never spoke of the "talking lighthouse," not even to Robert. And Robert said no more about it to his parents.

When Robert's leg got better, one day after school he climbed up to the lantern room. He told the lighthouse of the wonderful plans that were in store for her. Her dream would soon come true. This was enough to stop her hurting. From then on Robert heard no more sad crying from the lighthouse. Now she stood proud, patient...and silent...waiting for her new life to begin.

CHAPTER IX

The day came when Robert and his family had to move from the lightkeeper's cottage because it was soon to become part of the Seashore Exhibit.

Robert made his last climb up the winding staircase to say goodbye. As he neared the top, he wondered why his parents had never asked him again about the talking lighthouse. Did they believe him or not? Anyway he was glad they didn't tell anyone else.

When he reached the lantern room and once more viewed the bay, the ocean, and the island he had grown to love, he had mixed feelings of sadness and happiness. Sad, because he was moving away and would miss his friend. Happy, because the workmen would be here soon to make her look brand new.

He sat on the floor in his usual place and looked up at the unlighted lamp. Then he spoke. "Lighthouse, I've come to say goodbye. We've had good times together. I'm happy for your new life. I tried to keep our secret about our talks but I had to tell my parents so that they could get help for you. They don't say any more to me about our talks and I don't say any more to them. Lighthouse, do you think they believe me?"

Robert waited, but there was silence.

He looked for a faint flicker from the lamp...nothing.

"Lighthouse! Lighthouse! Can you hear me?"

He sat on the floor in his usual place and looked up at the unlighted lamp.

Robert slowly walked down the 192 steps for the last time. He knew that he would hear the voice of the lighthouse no more. But he had a warm, calm feeling that she was saying thank you even though her power to speak was gone. He knew that whatever gave the lighthouse this power, took it away now because she didn't need it any more. Her wish had come true. She would soon be restored.
HER LIGHT WOULD SHINE AGAIN!

The End

EPILOGUE

At exactly 9:00 P.M. on Sunday night, May 25, 1986, the Lighthouse was relighted and the blinking strobe light on the brick tower in the nearby state park was turned off. Once again the Fire Island Lighthouse was entered by the Coast Guard on the official navigational charts as one of the more important light stations of the Atlantic Coast. During the all-day celebration, the lightkeeper's cottage was dedicated and opened to the public as the Visitor Information and Exhibit Center to teach the values of our nautical heritage.

The glorious Relighting Day program was one of the largest celebrations ever held on Long Island. Thousands of people along the shore cheered. Hundreds of boats in Great South Bay and the Atlantic Ocean joined in by sounding their horns and noisemakers, and sending off fireworks. It was a day that will be remembered by all who attended— especially Robert Norris.

Acknowledgments

• To Luis E. Bejarano, a Director of the Fire Island Lighthouse Preservation Society, who suggested that I write this book and encouraged me to put into the story thoughts to inspire young people.

• To Rockwell and Audrey Norris, and their son, Robert, for sharing their experiences while stationed at the Fire Island Lighthouse.

• To Nancy Howell and Ann Bonner, National Park Service Rangers, who contributed important information about the history of the lighthouse.

• To Henry R. Bang, Long Island Historian and leader in worthy causes, whose book, "The Story of the Fire Island Light," was a most helpful reference.

• To Jean Wood, who drew from her experience as a children's book editor and a longtime resident of Fire Island, in the editing of this story.

• To the late Harvey Lewis, without whom all the above could never have happened.

• To my husband, Tracy Logan, who spent long hours helping prepare my first drafts and supporting the book's progress until it was published.

About the Author

Photo by Editta Sherman

Vivian Farrell, an educator, writer and performer, has devoted much of her career to entertaining youngsters. For over 15 years she has written and performed stories for children in schools and libraries, on TV, radio and the stage, including Lincoln Center and Carnegie Recital Hall.

With degrees from Syracuse and New York Universities, Ms. Farrell has taught elementary school and conducted workshops at universities and colleges in the United States and Canada.

Many of her stories for children have been recorded in an internationally distributed album, "The Musical Storyteller."

She and her husband, Tracy Logan, live on the South Shore of Long Island, not far from the Fire Island Lighthouse.

About the Illustrator

Photo by Tom Potter

Christy Edwards is a familiar personality as she is seen scurrying around Fire Island, delivering her commissioned watercolors and collecting new material with her ever present camera. As a most observant native, she has been successful in capturing the mood and feelings of Fire Island as no one else has. Christy has participated in scores of island art shows, furthering her reputation with residents and visitors alike as "The" Fire Island artist.

Her art has been exhibited widely elsewhere; her most recent one-woman shows were commendably reviewed and featured in the New York Times and Newsday as well as in professional journals. Her identity with Fire Island is as recognizable as her talent.

A BIT OF HISTORY

Adapted, with permission, by Luis E. Bejarano from the brochure, *The Story of the Fire Island Light*, by Henry R. Bang, historian and a founding director of the Fire Island Lighthouse Preservation Society.

The Long Island Landfall

After the War of Independence and the great Constitutional Convention of 1787, the United States began to develop as a symbol of hope and opportunity for all the world. In numbers that were to increase for a century, ships from the Old World carried immigrants and goods to a rapidly growing America. With their great natural harbors and 2 waterways leading into the interior, New York City and Philadelphia soon grew into more important ports than Boston and the first landfall for the ocean-going sailing vessels of the day became the shores of Long Island. On the seas for weeks and months at a time, the crews of sailing vessels and their passengers must have waited with hungry eyes and tense hearts for the sight of their first landfall in the New World. For many of them, that first landfall was the eastern part of Fire Island!

The landfall, however, was as much a menace as a welcome. No man today can say how many of those early ships ran aground on the sand shoals off Fire Island, to founder and break apart in the pounding surf, snuffing out the lives and hopes of passengers and crew in nseen and unheard tragedies. The ature and location of the barrier eaches themselves were dimly known nd little understood by the European ea-captains. Further, the sand bars nat built up a few miles off the barrier eaches were forever shifting with the ver-changing ocean currents, a onstant menace to unwary travelers earing the coast.

It quickly became obvious to the edgling government of the United tates that some method had to be levised to help ships crossing the ocean o find their way safely to New York Harbor. Because of the great need for lighthouse on Long Island, President George Washington signed the order or the establishment of a lighthouse at Montauk Point in 1795.

The Montauk Lighthouse was a giant step forward, but it was only a partial answer to the problem. Almost mmediately, there were indications that another light was necessary on the south shore of Long Island, if ships were to be guided into New York Harbor. Many ship captains tried to plan their voyages so that they would approach the unfamiliar Long Island coast during the day. With the unpredictability of wind and tide, this was not always possible. Often those early ships, with primitive navigation gear, approaching the coast in bad weather after weeks crossing the Atlantic, had no idea of their position. Many vessels foundered in Long Island waters during the late 1700's and early 1800's. Perhaps the one that finally convinced the Congress that a lighthouse at Fire Island was urgently needed was the wreck of the *Savannah*. It went aground on Fire Island Beach on November 5, 1821, with the loss of the vessel and the entire crew of 11 people.

The First Fire Island Lighthouse

Shipowners clamored for a light at Fire Island to mark the inlet into Great South Bay where a ship could find a haven in bad weather. Also, Fire Island was about midway down the Long Island coast from Montauk to the Sandy Hook Light. On March 3, 1825, Congress appropriated money for the purchase of land on the westerly end of Fire Island and for the construction of the original Fire Island lighthouse. The amount: $10,000!

While the exact dates of construction are not shown in the records, it is known that work was completed and the Light went into operation in late 1826. It is also recorded that while the original appropriation was for $10,000, the total cost of the Lighthouse, the dwelling, the well and the lamps was $9,999.65. The $.35 was carried in "surplus funds."

The Lighthouse was originally equipped with "eighteen lamps and burnished reflectors" and, according to the records, was visible for 27 nautical miles. It was equipped with the "most approved revolving plan," which caused the lamps to make a complete revolution in one minute and thirty seconds. It consisted of a weight attached to a cable that was hand-cranked every four hours by the keeper to bring the weight up to the top of the tower. A governor mechanism controlled the revolution of the lamps.

In 1842, the lamp arrangement was changed to 14 lamps and 21 reflectors with visibility reduced to 22 miles. There is no explanation for this. Perhaps it was an early governmental economy move.

The Second Fire Island Lighthouse

There is very little material available explaining the reason for replacing the original lighthouse, after only 30 years of operation, with the much larger present structure. Some evidence indicates that the original structure was not tall enough for its beam to be seen far enough to give the required protection to ships at sea. We also know that the first lighthouse did not stand up well to the fierce elements of wind and sea.

Many shipwrecks continued to occur along the entire south shore of Long

Island after the first light was placed in operation at Fire Island in 1826. The barque *Elizabeth* was wrecked near Point of Woods with a loss of ten people on July 19, 1850. Among the victims was Margaret Fuller, a well known writer, her husband and their young son. "It is a time that the United States, instead of keeping troops and forts, should keep a coast guard of lighthouses to defend lives and property," Ralph Waldo Emerson, speaking for many of the critics, is quoted as saying. There is some indication that the captain of the *Elizabeth* mistook the Fire Island Light for the Cape May Light. In any case, pressure increased for upgrading of the system of Long Island lighthouses.

The Federal Government moved quickly to upgrade the light service of the nation from one of the worst in the world to one of the best. Congress voted funds for the most modern structures, with the latest improvements in lenses, reflectors and lamps. The whole coastal situation was restudied, and a decision made to provide better coverage on the south shore of Long Island. This included the rebuilding of the Fire Island Light with a much higher structure and a more powerful light.

On March 3, 1857, Congress appropriated $40,000 for the construction of a new Fire Island Lighthouse, to be 168 feet high! It was to have a first-order Fresnel light, which would be visible for at least 21 miles at sea. Construction of the light which stands today was started in 1857. It went into operation on November 1, 1858.

The new light is built on a stone platform that is 100 feet by 150 feet. The tower is constructed of brick, circular in shape, with the walls at the base almost 11 feet thick, tapering to 2½ feet at the parapet. The staircase and railing are iron, with nine landings. The parapet deck is of granite with an iron railing. The 14 lamps were similar to those used in the original lighthouse. The improvement in the illuminating apparatus was the installation of a first-order Fresnel system, which greatly increased the intensity of the light. In the Fresnel system the lamp is surrounded with a series of prismatic rings of glass, each cut mathematically so that all of the rays are bent to go out in one plane.

As planned, the new light was exhibited on November 1, 1858.

From Light and Heroism to Darkness and Deterioration

For more than a century thereafter the Lighthouse saved hundreds of ships and thousands of lives as it guided ocean-going vessels to New York and protected smaller craft on the Great South Bay. The historic structure continued to cast light on an era of our past. Its story covers times of great change in our nation's history. Its lighting arrangements alone give a flavor of its history: whale oil, lard oil, kerosene, incandescent oil vapor and electricity.

Long Island's historic landmark, however, the Fire Island Lighthouse proudly erected in 1858 as a replacement for the original and inadequate tower constructed in 1826, was doomed to demolition in 1981. Its navigational function had been supplanted by modern electronic systems both aboard ship and ashore. Its light had been extinguished in 1974. Once called one of the most beautiful of all U.S. lighthouses, it was allowed in the seventies to be deteriorated by the elements and the salt ocean air to the point where its exterior began to crumble and it became a public safety hazard.

So it was that by the early nineteen eighties, with no government funds available, the destiny of the once majestic and proud life-saving Lighthouse seemed to be inevitable extinction.

The Lighthouse Restored

It was at this particular point in 1982 that a group of Long Island residents stood up to be counted: they refused to sit idly by while their memory-filled great Light passed from reality to oblivion. Under the leadership of the late Norma Murray Ervin, then president of the Fire Island Association, and Thomas F. Roberts III, a banker from West Islip, they took determined action and persuaded the Federal Government that the Lighthouse could be restored and relighted to capture some of its nostalgic grandeur and usefulness of the past.

They pooled their own monies and sought funds from their families and neighbors to fund an historical and architectural study to be used as a basis to estimate construction costs involved in achieving three major objectives: to restore and relight the Lighthouse, to convert the adjoining Lightkeeper's Cottage into a Visitors Information and Seashore Exhibit Center, to rehabilitate the tower's environs in a manner that would protect the natural ecology of the area.

The Federal Government agreed to authorize the restoration program on the condition that the funds be raised from private sources; it assigned custody of the Lighthouse and its property to the Fire Island National Seashore or the National Park Service. The U.S. Coast Guard was invited to participate in the effort in order again to include the Lighthouse, once restored and relighted, in the nautical charts. Over 4,500 donors contributed nearly $2,000,000 to the project. Congress recognized the monumental effort by allocating an additional $2,000,000 to develop and rehabilitate the site and build public access boardwalks to the Lighthouse. The restoration construction under the watchful eyes of the National Park Service, the U.S. Coast Guard and indeed the whole Long Island community, proceeded nearly on schedule as the contributions were received.

The relighting was in May of 1986 and the restoration of the Fire Island Lighthouse was completed by the end of 1987. The traditional black and white bands were painted once again, and the historical landmark functioned as intended when it was originally constructed.

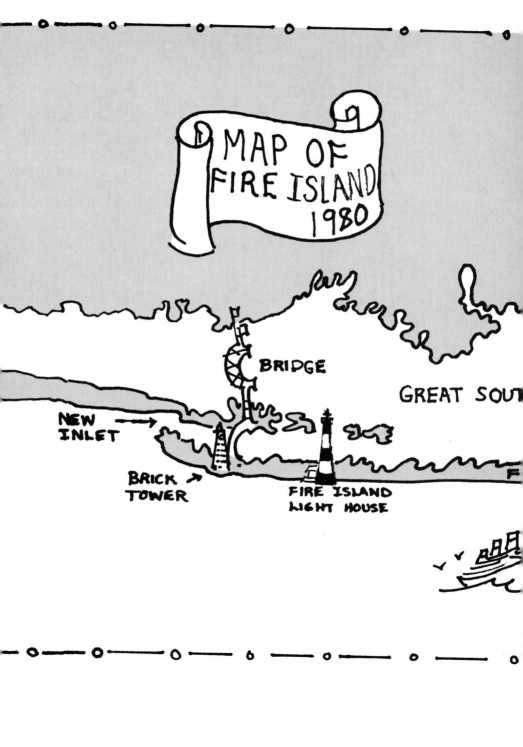

MAP OF
FIRE ISLAND
1980

BRIDGE

GREAT SOUT

NEW
INLET

BRICK
TOWER

FIRE ISLAND
LIGHT HOUSE

F

1622

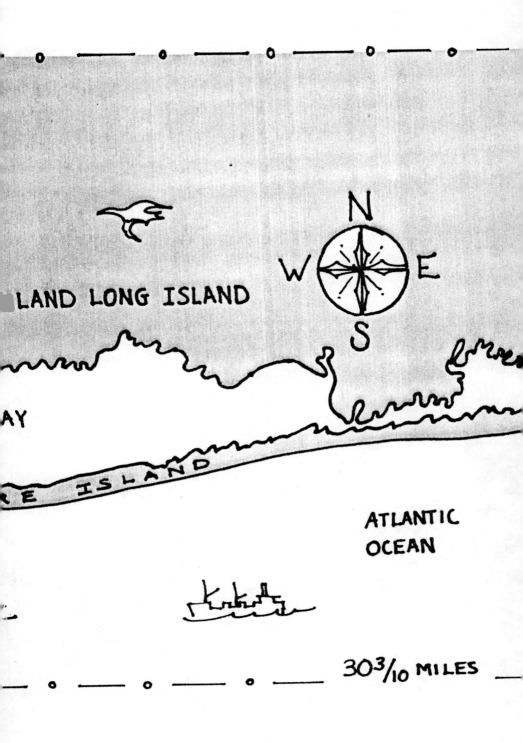

LAND LONG ISLAND

N
W ⊕ E
S

AY

RE ISLAND

ATLANTIC
OCEAN

30³/₁₀ MILES